D0537091

M

Is for

MISCHIEF

M Is for

Mischief

AN A TO Z OF NAUGHTY CHILDREN

Linda Ashman · Illustrated by Nancy Carpenter

DUTTON CHILDREN'S BOOKS

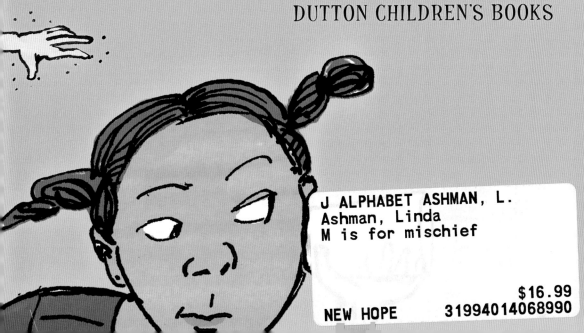

For Regina Alcorn, Jeannine West, and Shelley Lengieza,
three remarkably talented, creative, and dedicated teachers.
With much appreciation.
L. A.

For Maeve and Gareth and all the other lovable alphabrats
who were the inspiration for this book
N. C.

DUTTON CHILDREN'S BOOKS
A division of Penguin Young Readers Group

Published by the Penguin Group
Penguin Group (USA) Inc., 375 Hudson Street, New York, New York 10014, U.S.A.
Penguin Group (Canada), 90 Eglinton Avenue East, Suite 700, Toronto, Ontario, Canada M4P 2Y3 (a division of Pearson Penguin Canada Inc.)
Penguin Books Ltd, 80 Strand, London WC2R 0RL, England · Penguin Ireland, 25 St Stephen's Green, Dublin 2, Ireland (a division of Penguin
Books Ltd) Penguin Group (Australia), 250 Camberwell Road, Camberwell, Victoria 3124, Australia (a division of Pearson Australia Group Pty
Ltd) · Penguin Books India Pvt Ltd, 11 Community Centre, Panchsheel Park, New Delhi - 110 017, India · Penguin Group (NZ), 67 Apollo Drive,
Rosedale, North Shore 0632, New Zealand (a division of Pearson New Zealand Ltd) · Penguin Books (South Africa) (Pty) Ltd, 24 Sturdee
Avenue, Rosebank, Johannesburg 2196, South Africa · Penguin Books Ltd, Registered Offices: 80 Strand, London WC2R 0RL, England

Text copyright © 2008 by Linda Ashman
Illustrations copyright © 2008 by Nancy Carpenter
All rights reserved.

LIBRARY OF CONGRESS CATALOGING-IN-PUBLICATION DATA

Ashman, Linda.
M is for mischief: an A to Z of naughty children / by Linda Ashman;
illustrated by Nancy Carpenter.—1st ed   p. cm.
Summary: A rhyme for each letter of the alphabet describes the
misbehavior of a child, from Angry Abby to Zany Zelda.
ISBN 978-0-525-47564-4 (alk. paper)
[1. Behavior—Fiction. 2. Alphabet. 3. Stories in rhyme.]
I. Carpenter, Nancy, ill. II. Title.
PZ8.3.A775Maaf 2008   [E]—dc22   2007028491

Published in the United States by Dutton Children's Books,
a division of Penguin Young Readers Group
345 Hudson Street, New York, New York 10014
www.penguin.com/youngreaders

Designed by Sara Reynolds and Abby Kuperstock

Manufactured in China · First Edition
3 5 7 9 10 8 6 4 2

DEAR READER,

You, of course, are not the sort
To argue, fight, or brag.
You're not inclined to be unkind;
    you rarely whine or nag.

Others *aren't* so pleasant, though.
Read on, and you shall see.
Here's a catalog of naughtiness,
    presented A to Z.

Abby's apt to argue anytime and anyplace.
She'll argue over apricots, an acorn, or an ace.
She'll argue with an astronaut, an artist, or a waiter.
A shame she had to argue with that awful alligator.

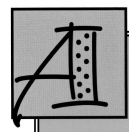

That looks NOTHING like me!

I said DRIED apricots!

You're a CROCODILE I say...

BLUSTERING BUSTER

According to Buster,
His bike came in first.
His bubble's the biggest;
His blister's the worst.
He belches the loudest;
He bowls like a pro.
He claims he's so bright,
He's beginning to glow.

He bragged he could fly
like a bird off the barn.
What bluster! Now Buster
has broken his arm.

CATASTROPHIC COCO

Coco came to camp:
Cracked a compass, smacked a lamp,
Clogged a drain, cut a tarp,
Clobbered Curtis with a carp,

Crumbled cookies, crushed a cake,
Crashed a kayak in the lake.
Called the counselor a cow.
Coco's cab is coming now.

DOODLING DAPHNE

Daphne doodles on her dresses.
Daphne doodles on her dolls.
Daphne decorates the draperies,
    the dishes, and the walls.

Daddy tells her, "Do not doodle, dear!
This place is a disgrace!"
Daphne waits till Dad is dozing,
    then she doodles on his face.

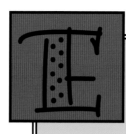VESDROPPING EVA

Eva enjoys hearing every exchange.
She creeps up to eavesdrop at very close range,
While people are eating, or out on a date,
At public events, or a private estate.

A whisper, an echo, and Eva appears,
Eagerly listening, straining her ears.
She'll sneak under tables, or lean from a ledge—
Uh-oh! Now Eva's gone over the edge.

Fiendish Frankie

Frankie flings a Frisbee,
Making Fifi flinch,

Flipping Fletcher's flan,

Frightening Mr. Finch.

Fifi fumes, "It's fiendish
To fling the thing like that."
Frankie flings another,
Knocking Fifi flat.

GLUTTONOUS GRIFFIN

Grandma makes Griffin ask Gracie to lunch.
Before Griffin greets her, he's starting to munch.
He gobbles the gherkins, grabs the granola,
Gorges on goulash and green gorgonzola.
He guzzles the gravy, devours the goose,
Glugs a few gallons of cold guava juice.
"Good gracious!" says Gracie. "You've gulped all the food!"
"Be grateful," gripes Griffin. "It wasn't that good."

HIDING HAL

Hal believes it's humorous
To hide himself from view,
Hopping out when people pass,
    to hiss or holler "Boo!"

How he heaves with laughter
When his hapless victims start,
Howling, "Heaven help us!"
    with a hand upon their heart.

One day he huddled in the hedge
    to startle Hank and Rover.
The hound, however, found him first.
Hal's hiding days are over.

IMPOLITE IRMA

Impolite Irma is ill-bred, indeed.
Interrupts Isabel, trying to read.
Infuriates Ira by popping his tire.
Imitates Ivan, inciting his ire.
Insults all infants, without provocation.
Irma irks more than an insect invasion.

JOKING JACKSON

How that joker, Jackson, joshes:
Hiding jacks in Joe's galoshes;

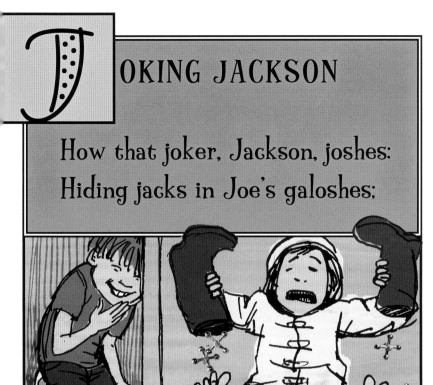

Jumbling jigsaws; telling jokes;
Tripping joggers; jabbing folks.

Mama's jagged nerves need resting.
Says to Jackson, "Stop this jesting!"
Jackson pledges, "I'll be sweet!"

Then smears some jam on
Mama's seat.

KICKING KEN

Kenny is the Kicking King:
Kicked the kite, the keys, the swing.
Kicked the ketchup and kazoo;
Kicked the fuzzy kangaroo.

Kicked the kiwi, kicked the gate.
Kicked Katrina, aimed for Kate.
How unlucky! Couldn't kick her.
Kenny's fast, but Kate is quicker.

LAZY LENORE

Lenore loves to lounge. She will not do chores.
She doesn't rake leaves, or polish the floors.

She won't lend a hand when Len washes dishes.
She lazily watches while Liz feeds the fishes.

She won't change the litter, or water the lawn.
Whenever there's laundry, Lenore is long gone.

While out on the lake, she won't lift an oar.
The boat springs a leak. Now who'll help Lenore?

MISCHIEVOUS MARTIN

Martin, at the market, munches macaroons.
Mops the floor with mustard. Mangles mixing spoons.

Mashes all the muffins. Marks the magazines.
Mauls the mozzarella. Mixes up the beans.

The manager observes him with a mild-mannered frown,
Till Martin takes a shopping cart and mows the melons down.

NAGGING NORA

Nora is nagging her nanny again.
"Nell," Nora noodges, "I need a new pen.
A notebook! A necklace! A nice little newt!
I need a new night-light! A navy blue suit!"

"Nonsense," says Nell. "You don't need a thing."
"I do!" insists Nora. "I need a new ring!"
She needles nonstop, till Nell says, "I'm through!"
It seems Nora needs a new nanny now, too.

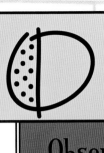

OFFENSIVE OSCAR

Observe Oscar's overalls, coated with dirt.
There's ooze on his oxfords, and oil on his shirt.
Yesterday's oatmeal still clings to his skin.
Droplets of orange juice drip from his chin.

Oscar's offensiveness grows by the day.
When ordered to bathe, he will not obey.
It's obvious, always, when Oscar's about:
One sniff of his odor and others pass out.

Grandmother

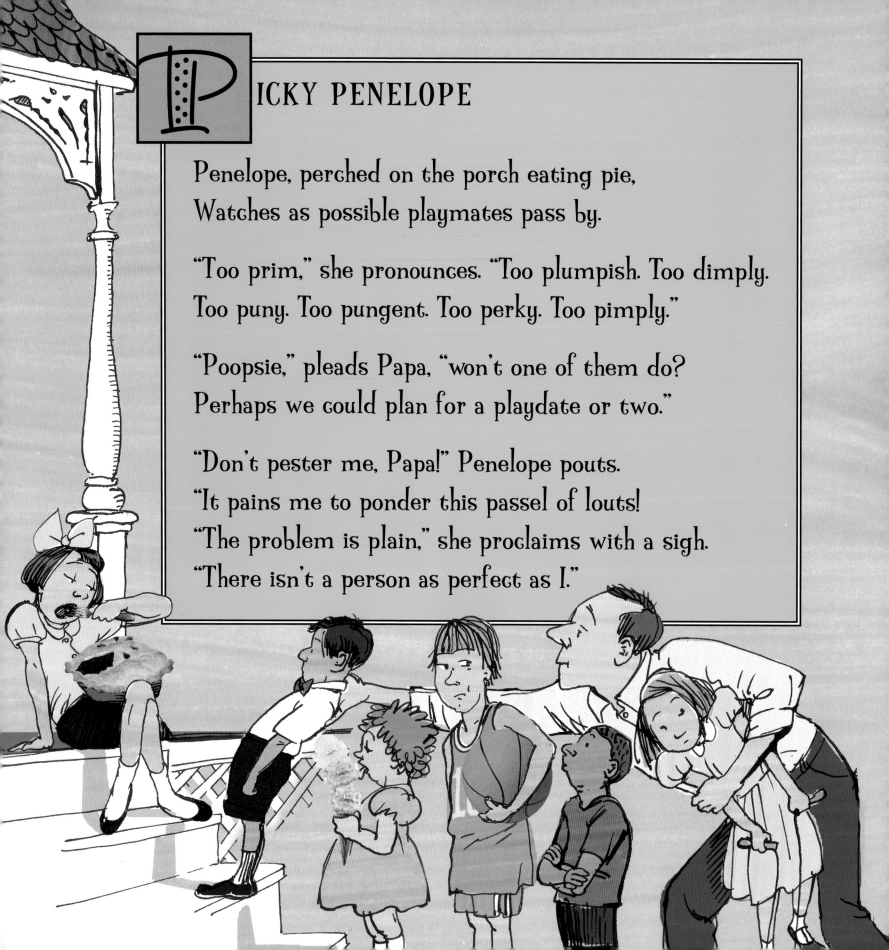

PICKY PENELOPE

Penelope, perched on the porch eating pie,
Watches as possible playmates pass by.

"Too prim," she pronounces. "Too plumpish. Too dimply.
Too puny. Too pungent. Too perky. Too pimply."

"Poopsie," pleads Papa, "won't one of them do?
Perhaps we could plan for a playdate or two."

"Don't pester me, Papa!" Penelope pouts.
"It pains me to ponder this passel of louts!
"The problem is plain," she proclaims with a sigh.
"There isn't a person as perfect as I."

QUARRELSOME QUINCY

It's quirky how Quincy is so quick to fight.
He quarrels with all, convinced he is right.
He quibbles with teachers, then quacks, "How absurd!"
He quizzes his classmates, then mocks every word.

When warned of the quicksand, he questions the scout.
He might quarrel less . . . if he's ever pulled out.

# RUDE RUBY

Ruby, at the roller rink, is raising quite a racket.
Rams right into Rita, then she rips Roberta's jacket.
Leaves a trail of raisins, calls Renee a rat.
Ridicules the music, steals Rebecca's hat.

The skaters find her rudeness too repulsive to ignore.
They spin her round and round so fast, she rolls right out the door.

SELFISH STELLA

Stella's so selfish! She won't share a thing–
Her scooter, her sweater, her soda, her swing.
She sprawls in the sandbox so no one can play.
She sits on the slide and scares others away.

Today by the stream, while skipping a stone,
She spied a small skunk that she wanted to own.
The skunk ran away, but sprayed Stella well.
She's sharing at last—too bad it's that smell.

TERRIBLE TWINS

Tom and Tim, those trying twins,
Trample tulips, topple bins,
Tatter tents, tangle twine,
Tamper with the turpentine.

Tackle toddlers, torment teachers,
Toss tomatoes from the bleachers,
Terrorize their timid sisters,
Trash the house like tiny twisters.

Mother says she needs a tether,
Wants to tie the two together.
Truly thinks the twins a chore . . .
Till the triplets move next door.

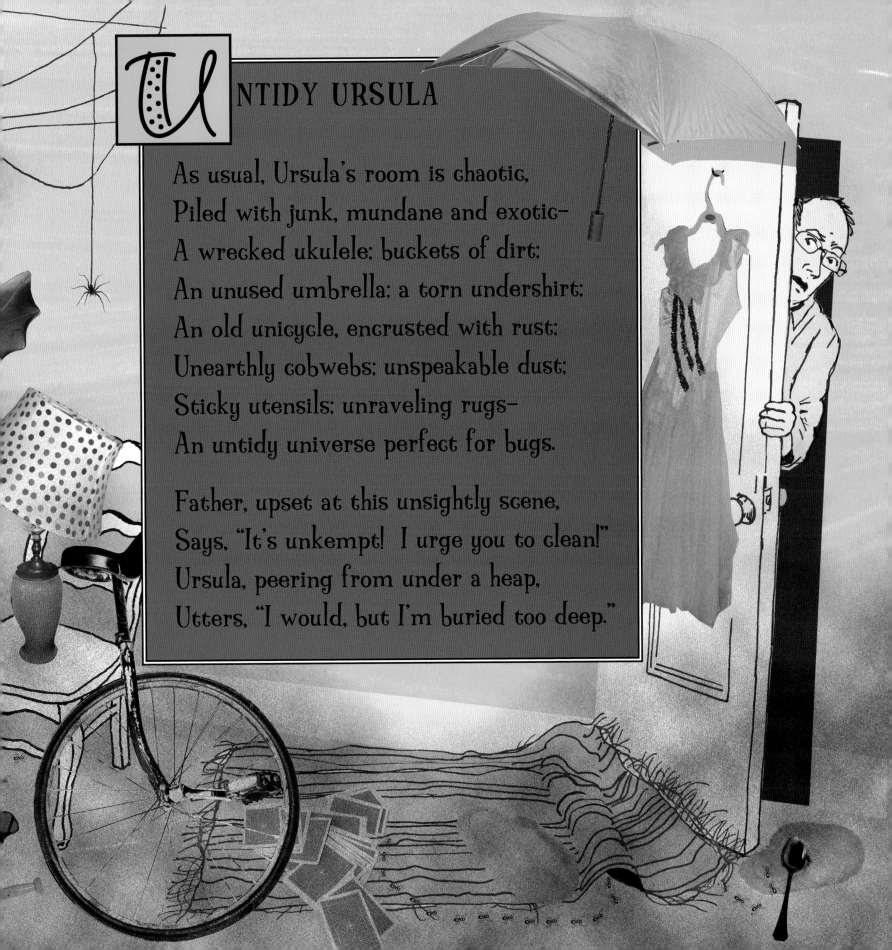

UNTIDY URSULA

As usual, Ursula's room is chaotic,
Piled with junk, mundane and exotic—
A wrecked ukulele; buckets of dirt;
An unused umbrella; a torn undershirt;
An old unicycle, encrusted with rust;
Unearthly cobwebs; unspeakable dust;
Sticky utensils; unraveling rugs—
An untidy universe perfect for bugs.

Father, upset at this unsightly scene,
Says, "It's unkempt! I urge you to clean!"
Ursula, peering from under a heap,
Utters, "I would, but I'm buried too deep."

VILE VERN

Look at Vern: he's always venting.
Vicious temper, unrelenting.
Vern's explosions, most volcanic,
Put his victims in a panic.

Aimed his venom at a snake.
Vexed the viper.
Vern's mistake.

WILD WILL

Will is at a wedding,
Wreaking havoc everywhere:
Waddling in the fountain,
Tugging Winnie's hair,
Wriggling on the dance floor,
Warbling through the toast,
Wrestling with the waiters,
Walloping the host.

The bride wails, "What a weasel!
Stop him now, for heaven's sake!"
He runs off willy-nilly,
Winds up wearing wedding cake.

X EXPERIMENTING XAVIER

Xavier gets excited mixing extracts in the sink.
Mama takes exception, says, "You'll make us all extinct!"
Explains to him explicitly, "You lack the expertise
To execute experiments as difficult as these."

Xavier exclaims to her, "It's just a simple potion!"
But Mama cannot hear him on account of the . . .

EXPLOSION!

YAKKETY YOLANDA

Yes, Yolanda yaks and yaks—
While she yo-yos, while she snacks,

In the yard, by the barn,
Peeling yams, knitting yarn.

Yammers till the doggies yelp,
Till the youngsters beg for help,
Till the yawning grown-ups moan.

Now she yammers all alone.

ZANY ZELDA

Zelda zips, Zelda zooms,
Zigs and zags through all the rooms.
Bangs the zither, flings zucchini,
Zings the zinnias with her beanie.

Dazed and frazzled, Zelda's mommy
Waits and watches, like a zombie.
When at last her zest is sapped,
Zelda zonks, completely zapped.

DEAR READER,

Well, my friend, we've reached the end.
And, now, for some advice:
Don't struggle to be perfect,
But—on most days—*do* be nice.

If you're nasty or annoying,
    rude or boastful, don't forget—
You just might wind up featured in
    an Awful Alphabet.